A Roomful
of Magic

Also by JOHN MARSDEN for younger readers

Also by MARK JACKSON and HEATHER POTTER

A Roomful of Magic

JOHN MARSDEN

ILLUSTRATED BY
Mark Jackson & Heather Potter

PAN
Pan Macmillan Australia

ONE

SAM AND LUCY had moved to the city. Their friends Naomi and Nick had moved too. They lived only three blocks away.

Sam and Lucy's house was made of dark red bricks. It was brand new, in a fairly new street, in a quite new suburb, on a very old piece of land.

Sam lay in bed at nights, listening to the growl of trucks going up the hill. Sometimes the house squeaked, talking to itself, like a baby.

There were no owls to be heard. No mopokes. No cockatoos stirring in the high trees and cackling in their sleep.

One night Sam heard a voice, crying. He could not make out the words, but sadness coiled around the room, like a streamer of smoke.

He called to Lucy, 'Did you hear that?'

'What?'

'It sounded like someone…well, I don't know what it was.'

She came into his room. She looked dark.

'What exactly do you think it was?'

'I don't know. It was weird. Someone crying. Or something.'

5

'Where did it come from?'

'Everywhere.'

'Well that's not right. Sounds are caused by vibrations. But you might have heard some echoes.'

Sam did not hear the crying again that night, and Lucy didn't hear it at all. But the next night it was back, and the next night and the night after that.

On the fourth night Naomi and Nick came for a sleepover. The four kids played Monopoly. Naomi won, like she always did. She had so many hotels they were stacked on top of each other. Sam came last. He owed the bank a million dollars.

After the game Sam told them about the noise, and they decided to listen. They met in his room.

Sam and Lucy's parents went to bed. The house got very quiet.

About half an hour later Sam gripped Naomi's arm. 'There!'

She nodded and leaned forward. 'And I can smell the forest,' she whispered.

'Me too.'

Gradually the crying got louder. Sam switched on the lamp. The children were perched on the bed. Sam looked calm but he was excited inside. Naomi was doing little bounces up and down. Lucy kept muttering, 'Captain Cook! Captain Cook!'

Nick gripped his pillow, and chewed on it like a dog with a rope.

Suddenly Nick whispered: 'It's under the bed.'

The children looked at each other. Their eyes were wide. The bed started trembling but it was just Nick, being scared.

'I'm going to have a look,' Sam said.

No-one tried to stop him, so Sam leaned over the edge. He couldn't get far enough to see properly, plus it was dark down there.

Sam gulped. 'I'll have to get closer,' he said, hoping they'd say, 'Don't worry about it.'

They didn't say anything.

Sam got down on the floor. At least now no-one could see how nervous he was. He peered under the bed. He saw the edges of a bright light, around a square in the floor. The square was shifting a little, like it wanted to lift. It started bumping and clattering. It seemed to Sam that it might soon blow off, except for one corner where it was sticking.

He couldn't stop himself. Curiosity can be stronger even than fear. He crawled in further and loosened the sticky corner. Immediately the square flew up, hit the underside of the bed, and skidded about two metres away, where it came to rest.

'Captain James Cook!' he heard Lucy shout.

TWO

SAM FOUND HIMSELF looking down an old bamboo ladder that disappeared into mist. A rich warm smell wafted into his nose, a mixture of moss and water and berries and animals. For Sam it was as though the aromas hooked a finger into each of his nostrils, and drew him onto the ladder. He didn't think for a moment about the other children.

He started to climb. The ladder was rickety but strong. Soon he was in thick mist. He lost track of the time he'd been on the ladder, but he kept going.

Suddenly the mist cleared. He was standing in daylight. At the same time the voice he'd heard in his bedroom sounded louder and closer. Sam stared around him. He couldn't see anyone, but there was plenty to look at.

He was in a forest of twisted trees. None of the trees was still. They shuffled slightly as they stood there. Creepers curled from one tree to the next, like snakes. In each direction the weather was different: bright sunlight, soft rain, fog, and in one area, what looked like snow. The night had disappeared, but Sam recognised the Magic Forest. He had returned

to the place of his
greatest adventure.

The feet of the
bamboo ladder were
just nearby, buried in
leaves. Sam noticed
the ladder trembling. Suddenly a pair of legs came
into view. It was Naomi. She was followed by Nick,
then Lucy.

As each of them reached the ground they stood
staring around, their mouths opening like pelicans.
Nick grabbed onto Lucy with one hand and Sam
with the other. 'Where are we?' he asked.

No-one answered. They were too busy gazing at everything. But now Sam paid attention to the crying again. It was still close but it came and went, sometimes strong, sometimes weak. Sometimes it could not be heard at all.

It came from the area of the soft rain, through a line of wrinkled trees. Sam took a few steps in that direction, towards a path.

With a great groaning the nearest tree lurched to its right and blocked his way. Clods of dirt rolled away from the roots and a thousand leaves fell.

Sam jumped back. So did Naomi, Lucy and Nick. Then Naomi came forward again and stood by Sam.

'The tree moved,' she said.

'No it didn't,' Sam said. 'That's impossible.'

'Well, what do you think happened?'

'I don't know.'

'How did you do that?' Lucy asked. She had crept up behind them.

'I just tried to go towards that path,' Sam answered.

'Trees can't move,' Lucy said. 'They have complex root systems. They don't have brains or muscles or limbs.'

'They have limbs,' Naomi said.

Sam tiptoed forward to sneak around the tree and onto the path. Almost instantly, much faster than last time, the tree heaved to the left and blocked him again. It towered over Sam, looking menacingly down on him.

'Captain Cook!'
Lucy breathed.

At the same moment the crying started again, in the distance, beyond the trees. Sam felt frustrated. He knew something was wrong and he had to get there and find it.

'Let's all go in different directions,' Naomi said. 'We'll confuse it.'

Nick was too nervous to go too far away from Naomi. But the other three spread out.

'Go,' Naomi called, when everyone was ready.

She charged down the middle, with Nick in her shadow. Sam took the right and Lucy the left.

But with a massive mumbling and grumbling and a heavy shaking of the earth, trees from everywhere thumped towards them. The children stopped so fast they churned up the ground with their heels.

'You know what's strange?' Nick said, but he didn't get a chance to finish. Sam interrupted him.

'We need a chainsaw,' he said.

The trees waved their branches like whips and Naomi smacked Sam on the bum, not for the first time. 'Don't make stupid jokes!'

'Okay, okay.'

'Did you notice,' Nick said, 'there was one strange thing…'

'Everything about them is strange,' Naomi said. 'We won't get out of here without help.'

'I asked for a mobile phone for my birthday,' Lucy said. 'And they wouldn't give me one. And now, when I really need it…'

'A mobile phone's not going to do you much good here,' Naomi said. 'We're in a different reality. I don't think you'd get a signal.'

'You know something strange about these trees?' Nick said.

This time he felt that the other three were half listening. So he kept going. 'When I spun around to run away they stopped moving.'

'Uh?' Sam said.

'Eh?' Naomi said.

'Hmm?' Lucy said.

'Well, when I turned my back on them they froze.'

'Do you have eyes in the back of your head?' Naomi asked.

'No.'

'So how could you tell they stopped moving?'

'I just could. The leaves stopped rustling and the branches stopped creaking.'

At first no-one seemed interested in Nick's announcement but suddenly Sam said, 'Everyone turn your back on the trees.'

'Eh?' Naomi said.

'Hmm?' Lucy said.

Nick made a gulping noise, like a surprised grandfather swallowing a large toad. He wasn't used to people taking much notice of him.

'Come on, hurry up,' Sam said, setting the example.

Reluctantly, nervously, the other three did as he said.

Peeping back behind them from under their arms, they saw that the trees had stopped all movement.

'Okay,' Sam said, 'now we're going to walk backwards down the path.'

'Are you crazy?' Naomi asked.

This was a question that needed no answer, like 'Why haven't you eaten your broccoli?' or 'How was school?' or 'Are you listening to me?'

Sam didn't answer it. He took his first few steps backwards, straight towards the trees.

To everyone's surprise, including Sam's, they didn't move.

The other three copied him. Like cats walking along a fence top, one behind the other, Nick and

Lucy in the middle, they made their way down the path. The trees were still and silent.

At the fringe of the forest Sam stopped. To his left he thought he saw an old man in a cloak, stealing through the trees. Sam frowned. He had seen someone like that before and he didn't like the memory. Last time he'd been in this forest he'd met a wizard who was dressed like that. But a moment

later the man was gone. Sam decided he must have
been looking at a tree, and not a man at all.

Suddenly they were in the open. They could walk
normally again. Now the soft rain they had seen was
misting on them. And just ahead was a young child.

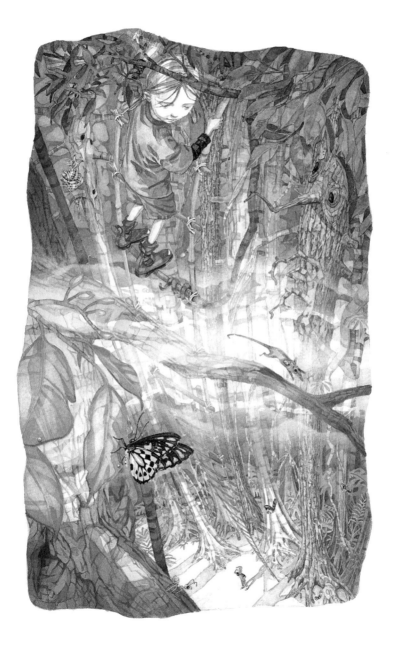

THREE

SHE LOOKED ABOUT three years old. Dressed in rags that hung like they had been through a garden mulcher, she was sitting on a tree stump, with two or three fingers in her mouth. And she was crying.

Sam recognised the sound. It was the noise that had drifted through his room so many times in the past week.

Now he went straight to the girl.

'Who are you?' he asked. 'Where are you from? Why are you crying?'

But she turned from him and would not answer.

Sam started to lose his temper. 'Oh come on,' he said, 'you've been crying for ages and I'm sick of it.'

The child slipped away and ran across the clearing.

'Wait!' Naomi called.

Already the girl was almost into the trees. But she paused. Naomi hurried to her and knelt down. At first the child wouldn't listen. But after a few minutes she seemed to soften a little. Sam kicked a pebble around the clearing and Lucy watched a beetle in the grass and Nick stayed close to some yellow-leafed bushes, hoping no-one would notice how nervous he

was. At last the little girl began to talk to Naomi. The words came slowly but soon she was talking freely, as Naomi held her hand and listened.

When Naomi came back to the others her face was grave.

'What's the story?' Sam asked. 'Has she lost her Barbie?'

'Lost her marbles,' Lucy said.

'Shhhh,' Naomi said, glancing behind her to make sure the child could not hear. 'You won't be laughing when I tell you.'

Nick drew closer, looking curious. 'What is it?' he asked.

Naomi took a deep breath.

'She was stolen from her home,' she said. 'Stolen by the fairies.'

'Oh,' Nick gasped.

'And what's more,' Naomi said, 'she thinks they replaced her with a baby of their own.'

'Captain Cook,' Lucy gasped. 'A changeling.'

There was a silence. The three children stared at Lucy but none of them wanted to admit they didn't know what she meant. And Lucy wanted them to beg her for the information.

Finally Sam said, rather ungraciously, 'Oh, all right then, what's a changeling?'

Lucy paused, to get her tongue in the right place.

'When the fairies want one of their babies looked after they sometimes change them for a human baby, and the human parents raise the child without realising they've been tricked.'

'Really?' Sam asked in amazement.

'I thought fairies were meant to be nice,' Nick said.

'That one we met in the rainforest the last time,' Naomi said, 'she would have swapped her baby for a jar of blackberry jam.'

It was Lucy's turn to ask, 'What one? Did you meet a fairy?'

'We've been in a place like this before,' Sam said. 'And yes, we met a rather selfish fairy. She helped us though, with her in-built torch. Gave us light when we needed it.'

Naomi went to the child, who had calmed down a little, and brought her back to the group.

'Where do you live?' Sam asked her.

The child did not answer.

'Where do you live?' Naomi asked her.

The little girl pointed. In a voice that sounded old and deep she said: 'Over the billabong, past the pepper trees, through the Quarrels and under the snowflakes.'

'Oh, well, that makes a lot of sense,' Sam said. 'Shouldn't have any trouble with those directions.'

'Sam!' Naomi said.

'How long does it take to get there?' Sam asked the little girl.

She didn't answer.

'How long does it take to get to your house?' Naomi asked her.

'One day,' said the child.

'And how do you get there?' Sam asked. 'Oh go on Naomi, I suppose you'll have to translate that too, before she'll understand it.'

'You go along that path,' the little kid said.

'Thanks,' Sam said.

He got up and nodded to the others. 'Come on. I don't know how long we're in this world or how we're going to get out of it but I guess we'd better get this little girl home first.'

'We're too young,' Nick said. 'There should be adults doing this.'

'Tough,' Sam said. 'There aren't any, not around here anyway. We have to do it ourselves.'

He set off. The others followed, the child holding Naomi's hand.

FOUR

THE BILLABONG LOOKED DEEP. Deep! It could have swallowed Uluru. You could have lost the Sydney Harbour Bridge in there. Throw a stone in and it would take a week to hit the bottom.

The children gathered on the bank. 'Why do they call it a bank?' Sam asked. 'Any money in it?'

'It's because 'bank' used to mean a shelf or a bench,' Lucy said. 'And the money dealers used to work on the bench…'

'Yes, well, thanks,' said Sam.

'How can we ever cross that?' Nick asked. He gazed fearfully at the water.

'If I get to that island,' Sam said, 'where those logs are, we could float across on them.'

The island was grey and wrinkly, round and bumpy. It seemed like one big rock, but with spots of colour, and driftwood logs washed up on the edges.

'There might be crocodiles,' Nick said.

'The logs might be crocodiles,' Lucy said.

Sam gulped. 'They might be,' he admitted.

He watched them carefully but they looked as much like wood as a log can look.

'I'm going for it,' he announced.

He pulled off his clothes, leaving them in an untidy pile on the ground. Then he splashed into the shallows, wishing he could think of another way to do this. Already the water was halfway up his thighs. It felt mysterious. He looked around at the others. They were watching anxiously. He hoped one of them would say, 'Hey, I just remembered this boat I've got in my pocket.' But they didn't.

Sam grimaced and launched himself.

It was like swimming in honey, soft and slow and heavy. He knew right away he was in trouble. The water seemed to want to swallow him up, drag him down.

After ten minutes he stopped swimming to see where he was. He felt troubled to find he was not much more than halfway to the island. Already he had little energy left. But he had gone too far to turn back.

'The point of no return'. He'd always thought that was a powerful idea. Too late to go back, you had to go forwards: the plane with not enough fuel, the thirsty desert traveller, the leaking hot-air balloon.

He struggled on. His legs were so slow now, and his arms so tired. He could hardly move. He knew he was making little progress. His head seemed to be filling with water. He felt it getting heavier. It would be easy to give up and sink.

A wave brushed against his face. It woke him a little. He swam a few more strokes. He glanced up. For a moment he thought he saw the old man in the cloak again, sitting on a wave quite a way ahead. Sam told his sleepy mind to stop being stupid, and to bring his arm over again. There was nothing else to do. He didn't want to give up, didn't want to stop, even though he knew now he wouldn't make it. Another stroke with the arm. The right arm. And another with the left arm. If possible. Try to bring the arm over. Try, try. No, it was too hard. Easier to stop moving. Easier to lie in the water. To lie there forever.

Another wave splashed against him. It splashed a thought into his mind. How could there be waves? This was a billabong, not the ocean. There was no breeze, no wind, no gale. Now he was lifted by a wave, and lifted high, too. He shook his head and tried to understand.

And then a huge familiar voice boomed around him, so loud that it turned him over and over three times in the water. The boy came up spluttering. He was awake now.

'SAM,' the voice roared. 'SAM! What are you doing here?'

FIVE

SAM HAD NEVER SEEN an island come to life before. It wasn't the first time the bunyip had helped him though. On a previous adventure the bunyip had flattened a horrible creature who was in their way.

Now he carried Sam to the beach to collect his clothes and the other children. When they were all aboard, they began their ride across the great billabong. Sam was so grateful to the bunyip that he tried to ignore his smell. 'You know,' Sam muttered in the bunyip's ear as they cruised along, 'we thought you were an island.'

'An island!'

The bunyip started laughing. Too late, as the children started to slide off his knobbly back, Sam realised it was a bad idea to say anything funny when riding on a bunyip. 'Stop laughing!' he yelled, grabbing onto a tuft of hair. 'Stop! We're falling off!'

'Sorry,' the bunyip boomed.

He stopped almost straightaway but for the next few minutes, as he swam along, he couldn't help but give an occasional giggle. Every time he did, the children were thrown up in the air. Lucy hung onto one of his ears, and Nick on another, and the little girl had a good grip on his third ear, but Naomi and Sam bounced high with every chortle. By the time they reached the other side they were quite seasick.

Nevertheless they were pleased when the bunyip announced that he wanted to come with them. Even

though he smelled like a fish shop on a bad day – a very bad day – and even though his voice was like a helicopter without a muffler, he had been useful before, and he might be useful again.

When they landed on the other side they explained their quest to the bunyip. 'Ah yes,' he roared. 'Typical of those fairies. You can't trust them. Nasty little things, fairies.'

No sooner were the words out of his mouth than there came a sudden rushing noise and a sprinkling of yellow and red lights. And in front of them was the only fairy Sam and Naomi had ever seen.

She was back. And she was mad. She turned straight to the bunyip and let loose a fireworks display of words that had the children gasping.

'Why you great bloated bag of bunyip,' she began. The words flew towards him like sparks. 'You waddling heap of compost. Of all the stinky pongy messes of poo I have ever seen squishing around this planet you truly belong at the bottom of the food chain. I've met dung beetles with more brains. Is that a nose above your mouth, or are you eating the rear end of a hippopotamus? Are they giant maggots between your lips, or teeth? Call those ears! I've seen better ears on a goggopuss.'

'What's a goggopuss?' Naomi asked.

'It's a creature on my planet,' the fairy explained. 'It's got ears like wet socks. Like a row of wet socks on a washing line. Anyway, who are these?'

Sam introduced Lucy and Nick, and tried to introduce the little child. 'The trouble is, I can't introduce her, because I don't know her name.'

'Her name's Madonna,' Naomi said. 'She told me while you were swimming to the bunyip.' She turned to the fairy and said: 'Don't take this personally, but I think she's been replaced by a changeling. And I think fairies are responsible.'

'I think fairies are totally irresponsible,' Lucy muttered.

The fairy did look a little embarrassed at Naomi's comment. 'Well,' she mumbled, 'childcare centres for fairies aren't up to much. But if it's really upsetting you I'll help you take her back.'

'Thanks,' said Naomi.

The little expedition set off. They went ten metres, then stopped. Sam had realised that they didn't know where they were going. He turned to Madonna. 'Which way now?' he asked her.

'There,' she said, pointing straight ahead.

'How do you know?' Sam asked. He was worried that she was too young to tell directions.

She didn't answer, just looked at Naomi.

'How do you know?' Naomi asked her.

'It smells right,' she said.

'Can't argue with that,' Sam said.

Off they set. As they walked along Sam thought about Madonna's answer. It wasn't too stupid, he decided. Home did smell different from any other place. Settling into their new house had been difficult. He missed the lemon tree and the woodpile. He especially missed the chooks, scurrying towards him, their heads down, little legs pumping away, squawking quietly but urgently. There sure were some smells when he cleaned out their shed. They were good pooers, chooks, and if Sam had been a bit lazy and not cleaned the shed for a while there were big piles of green and white poo. It made your eyes water. But the fresh straw always smelled good, so dry and clean.

The old house had its own smell too, a mixture of leather from the armchairs and burning wood from the fire and Anzacs in the oven and wax on the tables and roses in the vase.

The new house didn't have its own smells yet, and it seemed to Sam that it would be a long time before it did.

They were travelling through a bright sunny patch, but just entering a grove of trees. The fairy, in her usual wilful way, had flitted on ahead, and was fifty metres in front of the children. Suddenly Sam realised she was on the ground upside down like a fly that had been Morteined.

He ran towards her. As he got close he saw that she was lifting up and down every few seconds like she was tied to a string and being used as a yoyo.

But suddenly he too lost all control of himself. It was as though his bones and muscles were shaken in every direction. He fell to the ground and felt himself exploding in slow motion. He thought he was coming apart. 'What's happening?' he asked himself. He heard Lucy scream, 'Captain Cook,' and Naomi calling to the others, 'Don't go in there, stay back!'

Sam shot up in the air again and crashed down. He was heavier than the fairy so he hit the ground

harder. As he hit he heard the bunyip. It was impossible not to hear the bunyip. Everyone for five kilometres must have heard the bunyip. 'It's the pepper trees,' he roared. 'Sam's got the sneezes.'

Even in the middle of another whirligig roll Sam knew at once that this was true. These were sneezes so big that he just hadn't recognised them. This was not just his nose sneezing; this was his whole body and mind. Even his fingers and toes were sneezing.

He tried to crawl back but he couldn't stop sneezing for long enough. 'Am I going to die of sneezing?' he asked himself. He knew the others couldn't help because they couldn't come into the grove of pepper trees. He had to get himself out of this, him and the fairy.

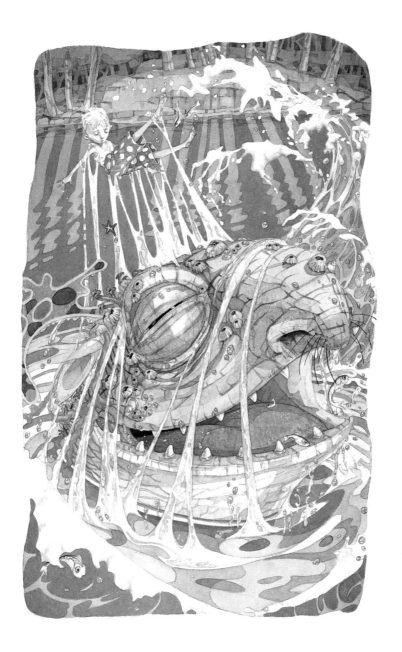

He lifted off the ground in another triple roll of sneezing, this time going so high he could see a huge bird's nest in one of the boughs. 'What kind of bird would nest in a pepper tree?' he asked himself. As he began to come down again he got the answer. A very small man popped out of the nest, threw a handful of black dust towards Sam, chuckled, and went back inside.

Now Sam understood. He felt pretty damn peppery himself. Here he was, his body almost coming off his bones with sneezes, and it was the fault of this gnome. Nasty nasty nasty.

He hit the ground, sneezed, and bounced straight back up again. This time he was even closer to the nest. He could see a whole lot of bones hanging on the branch. Human bones. 'So,' he thought, 'this is how the gnome fills his tucker box.'

The little man popped out again like a cuckoo from a clock. He giggled and lifted his arm. As he threw the next handful Sam blew with all his might.

The cloud of pepper went straight back into the gnome's face. A moment later and Sam was too high to see what was happening. He was so sneezed, inside and out, that he could hardly think any more.

But suddenly a missile went flying past him. Tumbling head over heels, the gnome was in the middle of the biggest sneeze Sam had ever heard. Soon he was just a dot in the distance and then he was invisible.

And Sam went crashing down again.

SIX

NAOMI LED THE WAY NOW, with Madonna hanging onto her, followed by Lucy and Nick. Sam was at the back. He had a Guinness Book of Records headache. The fairy hung overhead like a balloon with not much air. She too was sneezed out and had nothing to say. Only the bunyip was in a good mood. Nothing could stop him. Maybe a runaway train could, but nothing else. Well, maybe a normal train, but nothing else.

Okay, maybe a bus, but that was all.

Okay, maybe a kid on a skateboard, but nothing...

They marched on. Things were getting quite misty, and it was hard to see far ahead. Despite that there were several times when Sam thought he glimpsed that old man in the cloak again. Sitting on a low cloud. Staring from a rock. Striding through trees. Sam knew who it was. The sight made him shiver.

'What's that?' Nick asked suddenly, pointing through the trees.

The kids, bunched together, peered in the direction of Nick's finger.

'It's a froglodyte,' Lucy said, after a slow few moments of watching. Lucy just knew everything.

The other three turned to her. 'Okay,' Sam said. 'What's a froglodyte?'

'It's a frog creature that lives in a cave. Very old. You never know what they'll do. They can help you or not, depending on their mood.'

'Ah yes,' said the bunyip. 'Their mood towards me is generally not good. Not friendly. They spit.'

Cautious now, they moved forward together. The fairy had woken up a bit, and hid behind Sam. The froglodyte swivelled its head slowly towards them. It looked like it was made of stone, except it was rather purplish. Its eyes seemed to spin all the time, but it stared at them without blinking. As they got a little closer Sam realised it was quite icy. He could feel the cold from it. He decided he didn't like it very much.

The froglodyte opened its mouth. It sounded like a frog when it spoke.

'Bun-yip,' it said.

'Well, yes,' Naomi said. 'But a very nice bunyip, if you don't mind the smell.'

The froglodyte did not move for a moment and then suddenly a jet of spit flew from its mouth. It went straight for the bunyip. Slowly, like a zeppelin, the bunyip rolled over, trying to escape. The spit missed it by a centimetre and splattered into a nearby tree. White smoke sizzled from the trunk and the whole tree melted into a brown pool.

'Gosh,' said Sam. 'Impressive.'

'Gid-out,' said the froglodyte to the bunyip. He looked irritated at wasting a perfectly good tree.

'Why don't you like bunyips?' Naomi asked him.

'Stuck up,' said the froglodyte.

'Oh, but not this one,' Naomi said.

Meanwhile the bunyip had got to its feet. He was backing away slowly. 'If you want me to leave,' he bellowed, 'you only have to say so.'

'Shuddup,' said the froglodyte.

'Now wait a minute,' Naomi said. 'That's quite enough from you. I think you should learn some...'

She stopped suddenly as the froglodyte's eyes turned towards her again. They spun so fast that she felt held in their power.

'Manners...' she finished with a whisper.

The froglodyte's cheeks swelled. 'Help,' Naomi thought. 'This is where I get liquefied.'

The froglodyte drew back its head. Naomi tried to make herself roll away, like the bunyip had done. She couldn't move. Those eyes had turned her into stone. 'Maybe,' she thought, 'it's because I've got two eyes and the bunyip has only got one.'

There was a sudden rush of air. Naomi tightened up all over, waiting for the horrible stuff to hit. The sky went dark and thunder rolled around her like she was a ball in a giant bowling alley.

She opened her eyes. The froglodyte had gone and now a nice little pink cup and saucer sat on the stump where he had been.

The Wizard, standing behind the stump, picked up the cup and took a sip.

'Oh no,' thought Sam. 'The old man. The Wizard. It is him!'

His memory jumped to a previous time, when the Wizard, surrounded by insects, had turned Naomi

into a writhing white witchetty grub. 'Why does he hate us?' he wondered. 'I guess he's just mean.'

'Needed to be left a minute longer to draw,' the Wizard announced, putting the cup down again. He turned his gaze to Naomi and Sam and the rest of the little group.

'So,' he said. 'I have you at last, thanks to that little froglodyte. I was wondering when I would catch up with you pack of varmints.'

He spoke quietly but somehow that was scarier than a shout or a roar.

The bunyip had already backed off quite a way, to escape the froglodyte. Now Sam and Naomi and the others started to back up too. None of them dared say a word.

'Last time I seem to remember I wanted to turn you into insects, but you confused me.'

The Wizard was not following them. But he kept talking.

'Lately I've been spending a lot of time in the kitchen.'

He snapped his fingers. A cascade of glowing sparks showered around him. In their green light he looked for a moment like a skeleton. Suddenly he was holding a long stick. He pointed his wand at Sam, Lucy, Nick and Madonna the changeling. Only Naomi, away to one side, was out of his line of fire.

Now the Wizard shouted, and he sounded angry.

'Salt and pepper, sugar and spice,
Flour and water, noodles and rice,
Tea and coffee, butter and bread,
Apricot jam and lemon spread,
You're in the kitchen but you're not nice,
I turn the lot of you into MICE!'

Sam felt a buzzing all over and a twitching sensation behind him. He flapped his arms to try to drive the feelings away. It didn't work. He was startled when he looked back to see that he now had a long pink tail. He glanced down. Suddenly the ground seemed very close. His nose, his long pink nose, was just centimetres from the grass and his body was covered with white hair.

For a moment he felt weird but then he had a huge desire for cheese, and that drove away all other

'Salt and pepper, sugar and spice,
Flour and water, noodles and rice,
Tea and coffee, butter and bread,
Apricot jam and lemon spread,
You're in the kitchen but you're not nice,
I turn the lot of you into MICE!'

feelings. He looked around, nose sniffing eagerly. Cheese! Gouda, swiss, brie or parmesan, he didn't care. Brie would be nice though. Or camembert. He skittered away through the grass.

Naomi alone was left. She stood side-on to the Wizard, watching with horror as her friends and brother were turned so easily into rodents. What could she do?

SEVEN

THE GOOD NEWS WAS that the Wizard didn't seem aware of Naomi. He stood in the clearing rubbing his hands with glee. As he rubbed them, insects flew from between his fingers, big golden-brown wasps, like a string of venom.

Naomi knew she had to work fast. She took a step to the left, looking for a weapon, an idea. But the movement attracted the Wizard's attention. He swung around.

'OH HO HO,' he snarled. 'Another one of you brats. Well, I'll take care of you.'

He lifted his arm. Naomi was desperate. She looked down and saw a rock. It was about the size of a baseball. She picked it up and flung it with all her power.

She had no idea why she did this. Everyone knows wizards can't be killed, or even hurt. But she was so mad at the Wizard she did it anyway. It was pure wiz rage.

Whoosh! Naomi often played pitcher when they had softball at school. This was going to be a strike. Smack! Smasherooni.

Naomi had hit the Wizard's hat, fair and square in the middle.

It folded slowly in half, the air rushed through the hole, and it toppled off sideways. It hit the ground and lay there like a dead marsupial.

The Wizard stood gasping at her. On top of his head perched a small possum. It blinked at Naomi. Naomi blinked back.

'What are you doing?' she asked.

The possum huddled down a little. 'Sorry,' he said.

'What's going on here?' Naomi demanded.

'No-one took any notice of me when I was just a possum.'

'So?' Then Naomi realised. 'So then you took over the Wizard. You used him to do your dirty work!'

The possum hid its face but Naomi heard another muffled 'Sorry,' followed by, 'He made me do it.'

'Oh yes, very likely. Well, you just make him turn my friends back into people. Or fairies. Or bunyips, as the case may be.'

After a moment the possum whispered something to the Wizard, who rather sulkily muttered:

'Mice in the kitchen, flee for their lives,
From the people with carving knives,
Save these mice from nasty ends,
Bring them back like they were then.'

At first nothing seemed
to happen, then away in the
distance Naomi heard the
bunyip. A moment later
she saw him galumphing
through the trees and
with a whoosh the fairy
appeared from the opposite
direction. Suddenly Sam
stood up from a clump of
grass to her left.

'No cheese anywhere,' he
said, looking cross.

'Well, sorry,' Naomi called back
to him. 'Excuse me for not leaving
you as a mouse.'

'Oh yes,' Sam said, looking
surprised. 'I'm not one any more, am I? Was that
your doing? Thank you.'

Lucy appeared from almost under her feet, and was
followed by Nick and Madonna. 'Very interesting,'
Lucy said. 'The world from a rodent point of view.
Quite remarkable.'

'That was cool,' Nick said.

Naomi looked sternly at the possum. 'Now,' she said, 'you owe us a big favour. And you can repay it by getting Madonna here, who's a changeling, back to her rightful parents.'

'Oh all right,' the possum said. 'That thing there.' He nodded at the bunyip. 'Can you ride on it?'

The bunyip nodded. He seemed pleased to be able to help. 'If he doesn't mind,' Naomi said.

'And that fairy, can she give you a bit of light?'

The fairy nodded. She seemed less happy about helping. 'If I have to,' she said. 'Will we be passing any blackberries?'

The possum ignored that.

'All right,' he said. 'There is a short cut. You go through the Quarrels and under the snowflakes. It's that way.' He pointed. 'But go fast, and use her light as much as you can.'

The fairy smiled at that. 'So am I really important now?' she asked the possum.

The children ignored her as they clambered onto the bunyip's back.

'Giddyup,' Nick shouted, getting overexcited.

'I beg your pardon?' the bunyip said.

The volume of his voice made his whole body vibrate so much that the children nearly slid off again.

'I am not a horse,' said the bunyip. 'I am not a human being. I am a bunyip.'

'Yes, Mr Bunyip,' said Nick, hanging his head. 'I apologise, Mr Bunyip.'

They set off.

EIGHT

THROUGH THE QUARRELS turned out to be a difficult and dangerous path. The children did not dare to look to the left or the right. The noises either side of the path were dark and awful. There were screams and shouts, yells and yowling, calls and cries. The further they went the worse it got. Sam began to fear it would keep getting worse forever, that there would be nothing to look forward to, no brightness that they would one day reach.

The fairy's light was a little spot of comfort. She stayed closer and closer to them as the darkness of the Quarrels grew worse. But even her glow did not seem enough. It got very faint at times, and when that happened an awful fear came over the children. Would it go out maybe, and leave them all alone?

A finger scolded across Naomi's cheek and she bit her lip hard. She tried not to show her panic, because she didn't want to make Nick any more frightened. She huddled up to him. A series of screeches seemed so close that they could have been inside her chest. A hand wrangled across the top of her head. 'Captain Cook,' Lucy whispered from behind her.

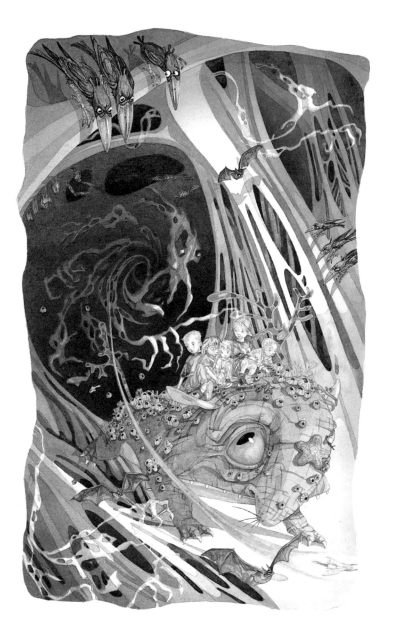

'Are you okay?' Naomi asked Nick.

'No.'

'Let's sing.'

'What, "Kumbaya"?'

Nick didn't seem too keen and neither did anyone else. The bunyip blundered on, close to panic himself. Further and further they went. 'I thought this was meant to be a short cut,' Sam thought. 'Do the Quarrels last forever?'

Then from in front of him he heard a voice, Naomi's voice. She had at last remembered a song she liked.

'Deep in the forest,
I know a fairy glade,
There in the cooling shade,
Sweet 'tis to lie.
Softly a dream bird sings,
Peace to the heart it brings;
Clouds drift on silver wings,
Far o'er the sky…'

The sounds around them gradually receded. Ahead was light. It was a long way ahead, but it was white and soft. The bunyip, tired as he was, managed to find a few extra revs, and started to canter. On his back the children struggled not to fly off into the dark and ugly controversies.

'Help!' cried Nick.

'Slow down,' yelled Naomi.

'This speed is completely unnecessary,' called Lucy, bouncing.

'Bunyip, please, get a grip,' Sam shouted.

'Faster, faster,' squealed Madonna.

Even as they barrelled along Sam looked at Madonna in shock. 'Faster?'

'Yes! I think I know where we are. We're near home.'

That got Sam excited too, and he started yelling, 'Faster, faster,' at the bunyip. When the other children realised, they joined in.

Until the bunyip started sweating. His speed got him so hot that huge drops of sweat poured from his sides. Suddenly he was as slippery as a water slide and he smelled like a wet dog who's been rolling in a dead wallaby. Even Madonna changed to, 'Slow down!' at that point.

But the fairy's wings were beating so hard that her light was on high beam, and the children could see the white of falling snow ahead. The sound of the Quarrels fell away and they came out into a plain of soft green grass. Above them snowflakes flew and fluttered. They danced in the air and the children grabbed at them. But each time, the snowflakes spun out of their hands. Somehow they never reached the ground. Sam noticed that the air was warm but the flakes felt deliciously cool when he did manage to make brief contact with one. Away to the left a couple of lambs chased each other in circles as the bunyip came to a halt.

The children slid gratefully from the bunyip's back. Sam went down backwards, over his bum and tail. 'Thanks Bunyip,' he said, slapping his friend on the rump. The bunyip nodded. He stood there, wheezing and panting. When Sam went around to his front he saw that the bunyip's one great eye was half closed.

'That was hard work,' the bunyip mumbled. 'Nasty place. Wouldn't like to do that again.'

'Well, thanks, mate. I think we'll be all right now.'

Madonna was leading the others across the field, through the lambs. Sometimes she ran, sometimes she trotted, sometimes she walked. Soon she came to a fence, an old wooden fence, and she climbed it quickly.

The snow stopped. They hurried on.

They arrived at a little clearing. There was a cottage with a TV aerial in the shape of a corkscrew, a vegetable garden full of corn and raspberries and beans, an orchard with apple and bubblegum trees, and a large well. In the vegetable garden a man was digging with a hoe, and a woman was pushing a barrow. Their movements were slow and tired.

On the steps of the house sat an infant, crying in a thin sulky voice. You got the feeling this child had been crying for years and rather enjoyed it.

'Mummy! Daddy!' cried Madonna. She ran towards them. The man and the woman looked up. They looked at her. They looked at the infant on the steps, who had suddenly stopped crying. They looked at Madonna again. Then they dropped the hoe and barrow and ran towards their child. 'Madonna! Madonna!' they shouted.

The kid on the steps got up and stared at them. No-one noticed her any more, no-one except Lucy. The others were too busy smiling at Madonna and her parents. They were proud of bringing them back together.

Suddenly the fairy child had a pair of scissors.

Lucy pushed Sam and Naomi apart and ran towards the house.

'What are you doing?' Sam called after her. He thought she said, 'Throwing the changeling in the fire.'

'What?' he yelled, and took off after her.

Lucy reached the child twenty steps before Sam. She knocked the scissors flying with one strong hit. She grabbed the changeling with both hands, slung it over her shoulders and ran on into the house.

Sam, now ten steps behind, was transfixed to see the infant's face start to change. It grew warts and hairs and began to age. It aged faster and faster.

Its expression became cunning and nasty and angry. It yowled at Sam. By the time Lucy got to the fire, Sam was frightened by the evil leering face glaring at him. Now the child looked like a monster, maybe four hundred years old. It was wriggling and fighting and battering Lucy's back with bash after bash.

For all that, Sam was horrified when Lucy reached the fireplace, ripped the punching and kicking changeling from her, and threw it straight into the flames, onto the roaring coals.

'Wait!' Sam called.

But it was too late. From the fire came a mighty whoosh, like a rocket. The changeling, with a noise like a cackle and a scream, took off. For a moment Sam got a glimpse of someone else too, a twisted dark shadowy figure that seemed as tall as the chimney. The two of them disappeared. The fire roared. A blast of heat made Sam and Lucy stagger back, coughing. They reeled out of the house. 'Captain James Cook,' Lucy gasped.

Outside it was as though nothing had happened. Madonna was in her parents' arms. Her mother and father were hugging and rocking her, laughing and talking and trying to tell her a thousand things at once. Nick and Naomi were watching, smiling.

At that moment Sam noticed the ladder to his room had suddenly reappeared, just metres to his right.

'Quick,' he called to the others. 'The ladder's back. Let's grab it while we can.'

Lucy and Nick scurried up it, followed by Naomi. Sam went last. As he reached the clouds he looked down. The fairy was in the vegetable garden, stuffing raspberries into her mouth. 'What are these red things? They're better than blackberries,' she called to him. Without waiting for an answer she grabbed two more handfuls.

Sam grinned and then waved to the bunyip. 'Goodbye! See you again I hope. Goodbye.'

The bunyip yelled back, 'Goodbye!' The volume of his voice shook the ladder so much that Sam thought it would fall. Hanging on tight he scampered up as fast as he could, till he was safely home.

For Oscar Charlie, the great great-nephew – J.M.

For Vasily, Garry, Tony and Carol – M.J. & H.P.

First published 2004 in Pan by Pan Macmillan Australia Pty Limited
St Martins Tower, 31 Market Street, Sydney

Text copyright © John Marsden 2004
Illustrations copyright © Mark Jackson & Heather Potter 2004

National Library of Australia
Cataloguing-in-Publication data:

Marsden, John, 1950– .
A roomful of magic.

ISBN 0 330 42129 8.

I. Jackson, Mark. II. Potter, Heather. III. Title.

A823.3

Typeset in 12/15 Janson Text by Liz Seymour, Seymour Designs
Printed in Australia by McPherson's Printing Group

Papers used by Pan Macmillan Australia Pty Ltd are natural, recyclable products made
from wood grown in sustainable forests. The manufacturing processes conform to the
environmental regulations of the country of origin.

12. Dezember

Die Stadt ist voller spannender Gerüche und Geräusche. Vor allem in der Weihnachtszeit.

Wie bunt alles ist und wie viele Menschen unterwegs sind!

Doch wie soll Soja in all dem Getümmel jemals wieder nach Hause finden?

Ich hab den Polizisten ins Bein gebissen, weil er mit seinem Fuß nach mir getreten hat. Und dann hat er mich einfach aus dem Auto geworfen. Unverschämtheit!

Wie gut, dass wir Katzen immer auf die Pfoten fallen. Das Polizeiauto mit Bruno ist einfach weitergefahren. Ich muss nach Hause, den Menschen Bescheid sagen! Aber wo ist unser Haus?

Ich war noch nie in diesem Teil der Stadt. Mal schnuppern. Wir Katzen haben ja sehr feine Nasen. Mhmmm, ein köstlicher Duft weht mir entgegen. Vier Kinder stehen vor einem Stand, in dem eine junge Frau mit dunklen Zöpfen, weißer Schürze und roter Bommelmütze duftende goldbraune Rechtecke auf kleine weiße Pappteller legt. Die Kinder sagen »Waffeln« zu den Rechtecken. Die Waffeln dampfen, weil sie noch warm sind.

Ein Kind lacht mich an und schenkt mir ein kleines Stück mit Sahne. Danke!

Ich würde gern noch bleiben, doch ich muss weiter. Am nächsten Stand trinken große Menschen eine heiße, dunkelrote Flüssigkeit aus Plastikbechern. Der Geruch piekst in meiner Nase. Schnell weiter!

Ich klettere auf den Brunnen am Marktplatz und schnuppere nach allen Seiten. Seltsam, nichts riecht nach »Zuhause«, nicht mal nach Brunos wuscheligem Fell und das riecht man meilenweit gegen den Wind! Mein Frauchen würde jetzt sagen: »Frag deinen Bauch.«

Also frage ich ihn: »Lieber Bauch, wo geht es nach Hause?«

Ich kann seine Antwort nicht hören, denn in diesem Moment fängt vor dem Brunnen eine Gruppe von Menschen an, ein Weihnachtslied zu trompeten. Erschrocken mache ich einen Satz und lande auf einem Kinderwagen. Die Decke ist weich und kuschelig und das Baby unter der Decke lacht mich an, doch die Frau, der der Wagen und das Baby gehören, scheucht mich fort.

Ich laufe weiter bis zur nächsten Hausecke, an der die Musik nur noch ganz leise zu hören ist. Meine Pfoten sind inzwischen so kalt geworden, dass es weh tut.

»Lieber Bauch, wo geht es lang?«, frage ich noch mal.

»An der Apotheke links«, sagt eine Stimme in meinem Kopf. War das mein Bauch? Kann er wirklich sprechen?

Ich laufe bis zur Apotheke und schaue mich um. Da höre ich eine Frauenstimme sagen: »Kätzchen, Schätzchen, was machst du denn hier? Komm, spring auf!«

Es ist die Nachbarin, die Bruno für einen Außerirdischen gehalten hat. Ich springe auf ihren Rollator auf.

»Wir sind gleich da«, sagt sie und schiebt los.

»Danke, Bauch!«, flüstere ich leise.

13. Dezember

Ein Tag auf einer Polizeiwache ist spannend. Vor allem, wenn man selbst eingesperrt wird!

Brunos neuer Zellennachbar sieht allerdings ziemlich gefährlich aus.

Ob Bruno hier heil wieder rauskommt?

14. Dezember

Bruno ist wieder da! Soja freut sich wie eine Schneekönigin.

Doch die Freude beruht nicht auf Gegenseitigkeit, denn schließlich ist Soja ja schuld an Brunos Nacht im Knast.

Oder wo war noch mal die Henne und wo das Ei?

15. Dezember

Soja ist verschwunden!

Bestimmt hat sie der Säbelzahntiger geholt, der auf dem Dach lauert. Er ist so riesig, dass seine Zähne bis über den Balkon ragen.

Wird es Bruno gelingen, Soja aus den Fängen des Untiers zu befreien?

16. Dezember

Soja will nach Indien. Und so wie es aussieht, ist das nur einen Katzensprung entfernt.

Warum hat sie das nicht früher gewusst?

Sie freut sich auf ihr Frauchen und auf ihr Zuhause. Doch der Weg dorthin ist gefährlicher als gedacht.

17. Dezember

Außer einem Riesenschrecken hat Soja zum Glück nichts abgekriegt.

Trotzdem hat sie keine Lust, heute auch nur eine Pfote vor die Tür zu setzen.

Als Bruno dann auch noch ein Versteck mit vielen bunten Paketen findet, wird der Tag das reinste Fest. Fragt sich nur, für wen.

18. Dezember

War das ein Chaos gestern!

Zur Strafe müssen Bruno und Soja heute mucksmäus-
chenstill auf ihrer Decke liegen.

Kann man im Liegen Spaß haben? Oh ja, man kann!

Ich fass' es nicht! Das kann doch wohl nicht wahr sein!«, wiederholt Brunos Frauchen seit gestern ununterbrochen. Mein Frauchen nennt so was ein Mantra, wenn man wieder und wieder das Gleiche sagt. Mantren machen gute Gefühle und erschaffen eine schöne Wirklichkeit, sagt Frauchen.

»Das kann doch wohl nicht wahr sein!« und »Ich fass' es nicht!«, scheinen die Mantren von Brunos Frauchen zu sein. Sie sieht allerdings nicht so aus, als hätte sie gute Gefühle dabei. Und überhaupt scheint sie etwas verwirrt heute: Sie hat Brunos Herrchen heute Morgen einen Toast machen wollen und stattdessen die Topflappen in den Toaster gesteckt. Und Tommi und Tina hat sie statt Ketchup einen dicken Klecks rosa Spülmittel auf die Fischstäbchen gedrückt!

Zu Bruno und mir ist sie seit gestern sehr streng. Sehr, sehr streng. Wenn sich einer von uns auch nur *kratzt*, straft sie uns mit Blicken, bei denen ich glatt wieder in Ohnmacht fallen könnte. Mir ist sooo langweilig! Bruno auch. Was sollen wir bloß machen?

»Ich *fass'* es nicht«, murmelt Bruno.

Ich muss grinsen. »Im *Keller* brennt Licht!«, reime ich.

»Da ist ein Gesicht!«, variiert Bruno.

»Ob das das *Christkind* ist?«, wispere ich zurück..

»Ich *weiß* es nicht!«

Bruno und ich grinsen uns an. Das macht Spaß!

Ich fahre fort: »Das *darf* doch wohl nicht *wahr* sein!«

Er: »Wer *kommt* denn da zur *Tür* rein?«

»Das muss 'ne *Katze* sein!«

»Oder ein *Hundebein*!«

»Es bringt *Geschenke* mit!«

»Und es ist ganz schön *fit*!«

»Ist das Paket für *mich*?«

»Du hast ja wohl 'nen *Stich*!«

»Ich glaub, ich *fass'* es nicht!«

»Das Christkind bringt ein *Sparschwein*!«

Wir prusten los.

Er: »Da kommen *Wünsche* rein.«

»Und manche *werden* wahr.«

»Das ist doch *sonnenklar*!«

»Und was das *Schönste* ist ...«

Ich überlege schnell. Was ist denn eigentlich das Schönste an Weihnachten?

»Dass du mein *Freu-heund* bist!« Hab ich das gerade wirklich gesagt? Sind wir Freunde?

Bruno und ich schauen uns an. Und gleich wieder weg. Ich werde rot, als hätte jemand Ketchup auf meine Wangen geschmiert. Mit Seife.

19. Dezember

Bruno ist nervös, denn Soja behauptet, sie hätte schon ein Geschenk für ihn. Und zwar ein perfektes Geschenk.

Was macht man, wenn man überhaupt keine Idee hat, was man dem anderen schenken soll? Und dann auch noch etwas Perfektes!

Brunos graue Zellen laufen heiß.

Jetzt brauche ich auch noch ein Geschenk! Bis gerade eben habe ich in aller Seelenruhe mein Mittagsschläfchen gemacht, da weckt mich Soja mit einem Jubelschrei: »Ich hab's! Ich habe das perfekte Geschenk für dich!«

Auch das noch! Ich habe kein Geschenk für sie. Ich hatte nicht mal *vor*, ihr was zu schenken! Ich habe noch nie jemandem was geschenkt, geschweige denn einer Katze! Bis vor 18 Tagen *gab* es diese Katze noch nicht einmal in meinem Leben – und jetzt soll ich ihr etwas schenken?!

Drei Minuten lang zermartere ich mein Gehirn, aber es fällt mir nichts ein. Und ich weiß, dass ich noch *300* Minuten lang überlegen kann … mit dem gleichen Ergebnis. Wer hat eigentlich diese ganze Schenkerei erfunden?

Das Christkind doch ganz bestimmt nicht. Das lag doch ganz unschuldig in seiner Krippe! Wenn ich die ganze Sache richtig verstanden habe, dann kamen die Heiligen Drei Könige mit Geschenken zum Stall, als das Christkind geboren wurde. Aber in der Geschichte, die die Menschen erzählen, ist in keinster Weise die Rede davon, dass das Christkind den Heiligen Drei Königen etwas *zurück* schenkt, oder? Eben. Warum dann ich?

»Was schenkst du mir denn?«, kommt es von der Seite angeschnurrt, als hätte Soja meine Gedanken erraten.

»Einen Maulkorb«, brumme ich. »Oder eine Nagel-schere.«

»Wie bitte?!«, Sojas Stimme klingt leicht hysterisch. »Ich will keinen Maulkorb und auch keine Nagelschere! Das ist ja das Oberletzte! Ein bisschen mehr Mühe könn-test du dir schon geben! Immerhin habe ich mir einen ganzen Adventskalender für dich ausgedacht!«

»Ich habe dich nicht drum gebeten«, schnappe ich zu-rück. Und wäre froh, wenn wir ganz schnell das Thema wechselten, denn in der Aufregung der letzten Tage hat Soja das Ding vergessen. Zu früh gefreut. Sie schleift etwas aus Tommis Zimmer an, das aussieht wie eine Gummiversion des Planeten Saturn: ein runder blauer Ball, ungefähr so groß wie ein Fußball, mit einer roten Plastikscheibe drumherum.

»Steig auf«, sagt sie. »Na, mach schon, steig auf!«

Mit einem strengen Blick lotst sie mich auf diesen Pla-neten der Qual. »Festhalten und auf der Stelle hüpfen!«

Sich an diesem Gummiding festzuhalten *und* dabei zu hüpfen, das ist ja wie bremsen und Gas geben gleichzei-tig. Unmöglich!

Mich beschleicht der ungute Verdacht, dass ein Ge-schenk für diese Katze zu finden mindestens genauso unmöglich ist.

20. Dezember

Christhund oder Christkatze? Bald werden Bruno und Soja wissen, wie das Christkind aussieht.

Aber was, wenn sie es am Heiligen Abend verpassen?

Eine Falle muss her. Nur wie baut man eine Falle für jemanden, von dem man nicht weiß, ob er vier Pfoten hat oder zwei Flügel?

Frauchen hat uns vor die Tür gesetzt, weil sie in Ruhe das Haus wischen will,»ohne dass jemand mit den Putzlappen Schlittschuh fährt oder aus der Treppe die Niagarafälle macht«, sagt sie.

Draußen ist Schmuddelwetter. Die Terrasse ist eine Seenplatte mit lauter Pfützen und der Rasen ein einziger, ekelhafter, kalter Sumpf. Wir drücken uns auf der Fußmatte rum.

»In vier Tagen ist Heiligabend«, sagt Bruno.

»In vier Tagen wissen wir endlich, ob das Christkind ein Hund oder eine Katze ist«, ergänze ich.

»Wenn wir es erwischen«, sagt Bruno. »Sonst ist alles für die Katz und wir müssen wieder ein Jahr warten!«

»Wir müssen ihm auflauern«, sage ich, »mit abwechselnden Schichten, damit keiner von uns einschläft.« Noch während ich das sage, denke ich, dass Bruno seine Schichten sowieso verschläft. Keine gute Lösung.

»Wir brauchen eine Falle!« Ich bin stolz auf die Idee. Bruno nickt zustimmend. Dass ich das noch erleben darf, dass wir mal einer Meinung sind!

Doch schon im nächsten Moment geht es wieder los:

»Wir buddeln ein tiefes Loch«, schlägt Bruno vor.

»Und wenn es geflogen kommt? Dann ist ein Loch sinnlos«, sage ich.

»Das heißt, wir brauchen ein Netz?«, überlegt Bruno.
»Tommi und Tina haben eins zum Volleyballspielen!«
»Aber wir wissen nicht, ob das Christkind hoch fliegt
oder niedrig«, gibt Bruno zu bedenken. Da muss ich ihm
allerdings recht geben.

»Dann locken wir es eben mit etwas Fressbarem!«, sage
ich. Damit löst sich die Frage nach Loch oder Netz in Luft
auf. Großartig.

»Ja, einen schönen, dicken Knochen«, fantasiert Bruno.

»Nix da, eine Schale süßer Milch!«, setze ich dagegen.
Das Christkind stammt von Katzen ab, basta.

»Knochen *und* Milch«, bestimmt Bruno, »dann sind
wir auf der sicheren Seite.«

Das hätte ich ihm gar nicht zugetraut. Mein Adventskalender hat offensichtlich auch seine grauen Zellen im
Hirn fit gemacht!

»Vor die Tür oder aufs Fensterbrett?«, frage ich.

»Knochen vor die Tür, Milch aufs Fensterbrett«, legt
Bruno fest.

»Gut. Und zur Sicherheit buddeln wir noch ein Loch
und hängen das Netz auf!«, füge ich hinzu. »Damit auch
wirklich nichts schiefgehen kann.«

Jetzt haben wir das Christkind im Sack, davon sind wir
überzeugt.

21. Dezember

Das Christkind sitzt in der Falle!

Doch es sieht nicht aus wie ein Hund. Und auch nicht wie eine Katze. Und es nimmt Soja mit!

Bruno könnte sich freuen. Da kriegt er auf einmal so ein komisches Ziepen in seiner Brust.

22. Dezember

Auf den letzten Drücker wird dann doch noch alles
fertig. Wie jedes Jahr.

Na, dann »Frohe Weihnachten!«

Oder etwa nicht?

23. Dezember

Endlich hat Bruno das perfekte Geschenk für Soja.

Aber wie soll er es ihr bringen? Er weiß ja nicht mal, wo sie wohnt!

Sieht ganz so aus, als müsste er noch ein letztes Mal sehr, sehr sportlich sein.

24. Dezember

Endlich Weihnachten! Alle atmen auf. Auch wenn Bruno unter seinem dicken Gipsverband kaum noch Luft bekommt.

Und das perfekte Geschenk ist auch überbracht.

Bleibt nur noch die Frage zu beantworten: Wie sieht nun eigentlich das Christkind aus?

Armer Bruno. Sein ganzer Körper ist dick verbunden, das linke Hinterbein geschient. Nur seine Nase und die Augen schauen aus den Verbänden heraus. Und das an Heiligabend!

»Lach nicht. Ist alles nur wegen dem perfekten Geschenk!«, sagt er. »Wo ist es eigentlich!«

»Da drüben«, sage ich und zeige auf die Wand. Frauchen hat den Schmetterling über meinem Korb aufgehängt. Der Glaskasten hat den Sturz nicht überlebt, aber er sieht auch so sehr schön aus.

»Die Menschen sagen, wenn ein Schmetterling am anderen Ende der Welt mit den Flügeln schlägt, dann passiert etwas bei uns. Weil alles mit allem verbunden ist.«

Es klingt schön, wie Bruno das sagt. So schön, dass ich lange nichts sagen kann.

Bruno grinst. »Indien liegt übrigens am anderen Ende der Welt. Nicht auf der anderen Seite der Straße.«

»Nein, nicht auf der anderen Seite der Straße«, pflichte ich ihm bei. »Danke, dass du mich an dem Abend gerettet hast«, füge ich leise hinzu. Und: »Wenn mein Frauchen nicht nach Indien geflogen wäre, dann hätten wir uns nie kennengelernt.«

Bruno nickt.

Mein Herz fängt auf einmal an zu klopfen. »Dann …

dann ist der Schmetterling ja das Symbol für unsere Freundschaft!«

Bruno zieht eine Braue hoch. Er sieht aus wie ein amerikanischer Filmstar. »Ich hätte dir natürlich auch einen Maulkorb schenken können. Oder eine Nagelschere…!«

»Schweig!«, kichere ich. »Ich hab auch was für dich.«

»Das will ich meinen. Mein Unfall muss sich ja wenigstens gelohnt haben!«, tut er empört.

»Ein Spiegel«, stellt Bruno fest, als ich ihm den kleinen rosa Taschenspiegel vor die Nase halte. »Und jetzt?«

»Was siehst du?«, frage ich gespannt.

»Eine Mumie«, sagt Bruno trocken.

»Quatsch. Den nettesten Hund der Welt!«, sage ich. »Und den besten Freund, den man sich wünschen kann.«

Bruno hustet, als hätte er sich verschluckt. »Hm«, sagt er. Mehr nicht.

Mein Frauchen kommt strahlend ins Zimmer. »Wir feiern alle zusammen Weihnachten, bei Bruno!«

Im Auto stupse ich Bruno von der Seite an. »Willst du wissen, warum das Christkind eine Katze ist?«

»Schnauze!«, sagt Bruno. »Jetzt ist Weihnachten!«

Dann tut er so, als würde er nach mir schnappen, doch um seine Lefzen zuckt es verräterisch. Lachend schmiege ich mich an ihn.

Frohe Weihnachten!